WENDELL THE WEREWOLF

WENDELL THE WEREWOLF

A FUNNY, FREAKY, (BARELY) SCARY ADVENTURE!

Written & Doodled by
DAN BOVA

WENDELL THE WEREWOLF

by Dan Bova

Copyright © 2022 Dan Bova

All rights reserved. No portion of this book may be reproduced in any form without permission from the publisher, except as permitted by U.S. copyright law.

For permissions contact:

danbova@gmail.com

Cover and layout by Ben Margherita

ISBN: 978-0-578-29587-9

TO H, G, AND LL

GLOSSARY

WEREWOLF:
A PERSON WHO TURNS INTO A BLOOD-THIRSTY WOLF DURING THE FULL MOON. (NOT RECOMMENDED FOR PLAYDATES.)

CHEESEBURGER:
A HAMBURGER COVERED IN OOEY-GOOEY DELICIOUSNESS.

BOOK:
THIS THING YOU ARE READING RIGHT NOW.

BORING:
WHAT GLOSSARIES ARE. LET'S GET ON WITH THE STORY!

CONTENTS

PROLOGUE	THE PART BEFORE IT STARTS	1
CHAPTER 1	MEAT YOU IN EEVILLE	3
CHAPTER 2	DIET OF A WIMPY WOLF	7
CHAPTER 3	MOON GLOOM	13
CHAPTER 4	COME OUT WITH YOUR HUMAN HANDS UP!	17
CHAPTER 5	THE ONLY THING WE HAVE TO FEAR IS FUR ITSELF	23
CHAPTER 6	A LOAD OF BULLY	27
CHAPTER 7	FAMILY SHAME NIGHT	33
CHAPTER 8	HAIR TODAY, GONE TOMORROW	39
CHAPTER 9	WORLD'S WEIRDEST PIRATE	45
CHAPTER 10	THE ADVENTURE BEGINS!	51

CHAPTER 11	WAIT, YOU CALL THAT ADVENTURE?	53
CHAPTER 12	SOME ADVENTURE PLEASE? PRETTY PLEASE?	55
CHAPTER 13	SHOCK AND PAW	61
CHAPTER 14	NEW YUM CITY	65
CHAPTER 15	THE FARTY BOYS	67
CHAPTER 16	TO EAT A MOCKINGBIRD	71
CHAPTER 17	HAIRY PLOTTER AND THE CAPTAIN'S ESCAPE	75
CHAPTER 18	CHICKEN SOUP FOR THE HALF-HUMAN SOUL	79
CHAPTER 19	THE FAST AND THE FURRIEST	83
CHAPTER 20	BRIGHT LIGHTS, BIG TROUBLE	87
CHAPTER 21	A HAIRY SITUATION	91
CHAPTER 22	DON'T GO IN THERE!	95
EPILOGUE	THE PART AFTER THE END	103

PROLOGUE
THE PART BEFORE IT STARTS

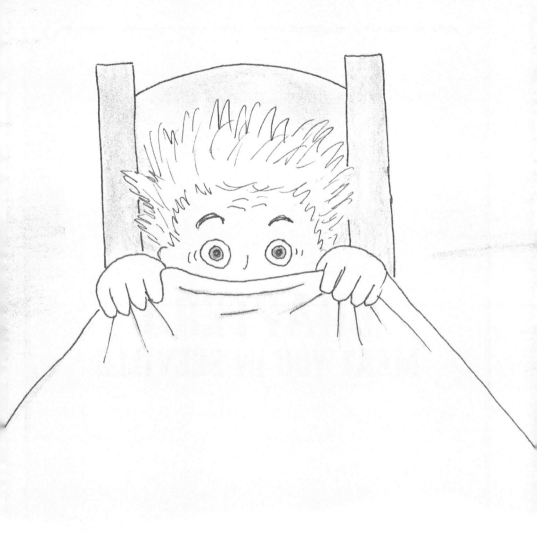

Ever have one of those cruddy dreams where everyone you know and love is trying to destroy you? And then you open your eyes in the morning and realize that you weren't dreaming at all, and everyone actually is trying to destroy you?

Hopefully you answered no to that question. But a kid named Wendell wasn't so lucky. Everyone was out to get him, and for what? All because of one very weird snack. Want to find out more? Then turn the page and read on to witness Wendell's super-spooky story. (But don't worry, it's really not that spooky.)

CHAPTER 1
MEAT YOU IN EEEVILLE

Welcome to the quiet, sleepy town of Eeville, where it is the middle of the night and someone is screaming her head off.

Okay, so maybe not so much with the "quiet and sleepy" part.

The screamer is Old Lady Fanny Fang. She woke up in the middle of the night and got out of her bed to go pee. Her relief was brief, however, because when she looked outside her bathroom window, she saw something that nearly scared the fur off of her…

Fur? Oh yeah, you should know that Old Lady Fanny Fang, like everyone else who lives here in Eeeville, is a snarling wolf. So if you walked around Eeeville and got hungry, you could stop at Taco Yell and order a squeaking mouse burrito ($2 for extra squeak). If you played baseball, you'd try to hit the ball with your pet bat. And if you were heading to the beach, you'd stop by Sunglass Hut. (Hey, just because you're a monster doesn't mean you don't like building sandcastles in style.)

The wolves didn't always live here in Eeeville. A long time ago, they lived with humans way over on the other side of Fog Lake. But the humans kept complaining about the wolves' habit of eating them (bunch of whiners!), so they packed up their things and moved across the lake to their new home, Eeeville, a place where they could laugh and play and swallow cute little bunny rabbits and squirrels without anyone giving them any attitude about it. Sounds nice, right?

Anyway, back to the screaming Old Lady Fanny Fang. What could a werewolf see outside that would freak her out so much?

A cheeseburger cooking on a barbecue grill.

Yuck!

See, to these wolves, cooked food is the most disgusting thing imaginable. And so Old Lady Fanny Fang did what anyone who has just seen the most disgusting thing imaginable would do: she screamed and passed out with a plop.

Cooked food…who could have done such a ghastly thing?

CHAPTER 2
DIET OF A WIMPY WOLF

News of the cooked food incident traveled fast around Eeeville. It was all anyone at The Wolf It Down Cafe could talk about the next morning as they drank fresh cups of Joe. (Joe was an insurance salesman who made the mistake of traveling across Fog Lake to try to sell bite insurance and wound up in a smoothie.)

"What kind of monster would cook food?" asked Wolf It Down Cafe owner Barry Blood.

"Was it a ghost?" asked Ricky Rip, looking down at his plate of ribbiting frogs.

"An evil alien?" screeched Sandy Screech.

"Since everyone is asking questions," said one of the frogs on Ricky Rip's plate, "can I ask if it would be possible for you not to eat me?"

Ricky plucked the frog off his plate. "No chance, hoppy." Gulp!

Ricky stuck a long nail into his mouth and flicked out a frog eyeball stuck between his teeth. "Cooked food, what kind of messed-up sicko would put something so disgusting in their mouth? Can you imagine?"

In a house across town, an 11-year-old wolf named Wendell had no problem imagining what kind of messed-up sicko who would do that: He was staring at him in the mirror.

Yep, meet the cooked-food-eating monster: Wendell Wolf, a shy, quiet, kinda short wolf with one little teensy, weensy secret. Well, it is more like a jumbo super-sized secret. Every time the pale light of the full moon hits his furry face, a terrible change takes place...

It starts with a kind of itchy feeling in his nose. Then, like a fire, it spreads across his face and all over his body. Every hair on his wolf body pulls into his skin. His pointy ears get unpointed, his claws retract into his fingertips, his drooling mouth stops drooling and his tail zips straight up his...well, let's just say it disappears.

Figure out his secret yet? When the light of the full moon hits Wendell Wolf, he turns into a human. Just like a werewolf, but in reverse. He tried taking allergy medicine to stop it, but no luck. That's bad news for Wendell because, oh boy, in a town of monsters, it isn't easy to be a boy.

Shapeshifting has more problems than you might think. Besides suddenly getting chilly without all that fur, when Wendell gets his human body, he also gets the dreaded Tummy Rumbles. An inescapable craving for deliciously prepared, perfectly cooked food. Sizzling cheeseburgers cooked medium-rare. Fried chicken fingers crispy on the outside and juicy on the inside. Sizzling pepperoni pizza. Oh, the horror!

Wendell kept this secret from everyone. He didn't whisper a word to his family, his friends, his neighbors, his bus driver, his plumber–you get the idea. He told no one. What would they say if they found out that a few nights a month, he turned into a hideous, hairless beast? They'd be terrified of him and probably throw him in jail for the rest of his weird life. Or worse, stick him in the zoo. Animals at the Eeeville Zoo didn't usually last long. The head zookeeper, Frederick Ferocious, once ate an entire flock of penguins and had brain freeze for a month.

Wendell knew he should stop sneaking out for cooked food, especially now that the whole town was looking for a monster who ate grilled cheeseburgers. But once the Tummy Rumbles kicked in, there was no way to tell his growling stomach "No!" Wendell was doomed...and tonight he was having another epic snack attack.

CHAPTER 3
MOON GLOOM

Crash went the back window of The Wolf It Down Cafe. Wendell's brain told him, "Don't do it!" but his belly bellowed, "Keep going!" Wendell hated when his body parts argue and came up with a compromise. "Brain, if you let me go inside and commit this crime, I promise I'll let you solve extra math problems tomorrow at school. Deal?"

His brain thought for a minute, then finally agreed. "Deal," it muttered.

"Fantastic," said his belly. "Now can we stop with the chit-chat and get with the chew-chew?"

Wendell reached inside and undid the window lock. Ouch! He quickly learned that his human skin is much easier to cut than his fur-covered skin. But that didn't stop him.

He fumbled around in the dark, knocking over cans of Sneeze-wiz, boxes of Spleencicles and Footlong Feet. (They were on sale!) When his puny human eyes finally adjusted to the dark, he found the giant walk-in kitchen freezer and grabbed his prize: stacks of raw ground beef patties.

Wendell smiled from hairless ear to hairless ear. Now all he had to was dig a bbq pit, build a fire, and grill away. He'd eat and eat and eat some more until the Tummy Rumbles begged him to stop. Totally awesome! Then, suddenly, the burglar alarm went off. Totally not awesome!

Wendell froze in terror, which is an easy thing to do if you're standing in the middle of a giant walk-in freezer. The cops would be here any second. His brain warned, "Drop the burgers and run!" But his belly was like, "Do we have to argue about everything? Stick a few in your pockets!"

Too late! Wendell heard paws stomping outside the front and back doors. The cops were here. He was surrounded!

Wendell would have had tears streaming out of his eyes out and down his face, but it was really cold in there and they were frozen to his eyeballs.

He could only imagine what his mother would think when she found out he was the human. Or worse, what it would feel like to be pulled in four directions at once by the cops. He could barely touch his toes during warm-up stretches in gym class!

CHAPTER 4
COME OUT WITH YOUR HUMAN HANDS UP!

"We know you're in there!" shouted Detective Sam Slay. "Come out peacefully, or we're coming in, um, not-so-peacefully!"

No response came from inside The Wolf It Down Cafe. This really bummed out Detective Sam Slay, who was totally out of breath from walking from his squad car to the front door. "Please come out? I'm pooped."

Again, no response. Now Detective Sam Slay was mad. "Fine! We're coming in and when we find you, you're going to jail forever!"

The police wolves busted in through the front and back doors of The Wolf It Down Cafe. One wolf crashed in through a window, just for fun. They stormed through the place, shouting and knocking things over until they finally found...nothing.

The place was empty.

"Hello?" shouted Detective Sam Slay. "Is anybody in here?"

"The crooks musta split," observed Officer Rita Roar. "Ooh, look, Blood Blast Boxes!" He reached down and poked the attached straw through the foil hole on the top. "My kids love these things!" Detective Sam Slay slapped it out of his hands.

"The crook could be hiding," he said to the police wolves. "Look underneath and inside of everything."

"Oh goody, I love playing Hide-n-Seek!" squealed Officer Rita Roar.

"Remind me to fire you tomorrow," grumbled Detective Sam Slay.

"You got it boss!" said Officer Roar.

The cops looked under every crate and behind every bag on every shelf and found two things: nada and zilch. As they began filing out, Officer Roar asked, "Detective Slay, if you are going to fire me, can we stop on the way home at Ben & Deadly's for a scoop of frozen chunky monkey?"

Detective Sam Slay stopped in his tracks, "Roar, you're a genius! We looked everywhere in this joint except inside the freezer!"

Wendell wanted to scream but figured that would be a pretty bad idea. So he bit his tongue instead and stayed in his hiding spot in the freezer: hanging off a meat hook in the middle of a bunch of gutted pigs. All he had to do was remain perfectly motionless, not breathe, and maybe develop the power to become invisible. How hard could that be?

Slay slowly walked toward the freezer, his slingshot loaded with a silver ball.

"You happy, stupid stomach?" asked Wendell's brain.

"If we get out of here alive, I'm eating you for breakfast," answered his very upset stomach.

Slay finally reached the freezer door.

If there was anyone in Eeeville more terrified than Wendell right now, it was Detective Sam Slay. Twenty years on the force and he had never faced a moment like this. Underneath his tough, burly exterior, Slay was panicking. Was a burglar hiding in there? Or maybe the cooked food monster? This could be bad! Like, really bad!

But it was his job to deal with whatever was waiting on the other side of that door, bad or badder. So Slay grabbed the freezer door handle, counted to three, and then screamed like a baby and yanked the door open with all of his might.

Slight problem. Slay pulled the door open a little too hard. Okay, a lot too hard. He heaved it open with so much force that it shook all of the pigs off their hooks. They crashed to the ground in a big pile of pork with a thunderous thud!

The thud, like a lot of things, terrified Detective Sam Slay who leaped three feet in the air, then did the only thing he could do to salvage his dignity: He screamed for his mommy and ran.

Luckily and unluckily for Wendell, he was at the bottom of that pile of pig-sicles. Out of sight and out of smell of the police wolves' noses, who followed Slay out the door, laughing their hairy butts off at him.

He was now alone and out of danger, but Wendell still couldn't breathe. Not because he was terrified, but because he had a frozen pigtail stuck up his nose.

He yanked out the tail, wiggled his way out from beneath the pile of frozen pigs, and snuck his way all the way back home. (Well, after he stopped to grill up some of the burgers he nabbed from the freezer–hey, he almost croaked getting them, it would be crazy not to eat them, right?)

He crawled into his bed and lay there, staring at the moon outside his window. He swore he could hear it laughing at him, mocking him. Then he realized he was sitting on his Chewy The Clown-Eating Clown doll. Wendell tossed it and went to sleep, hoping he'd wake up with fur and fangs like a normal wolf.

CHAPTER 5
THE ONLY THING WE HAVE TO FEAR IS FUR ITSELF

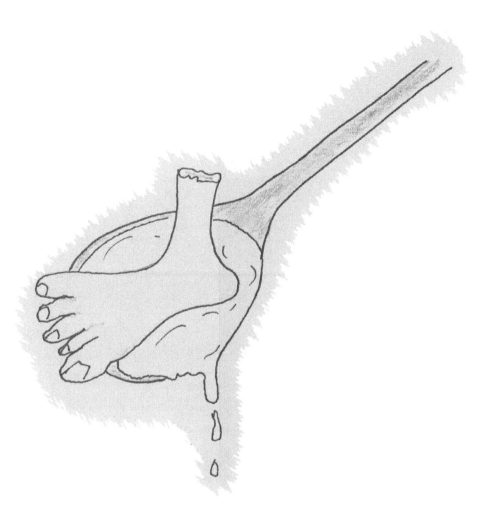

The next morning, Wendell woke up a wolf. Well, barely woke up. He was so tired he could barely lift the spoon to his mouth from his bowl of Shredded Mini Feet.

Wendell's Mom sipped at her mug of rabbit guts (which will wake you up faster than 1,000 cups of coffee) and Wendell's Dad had his nose buried in a copy of The Eeeville Post. "I can't stand these fat cats in the government!" he said with disgust. "Says here that they are raising taxes on eating fat cats!"

"Your doctor said you need to cut back on those anyway," said Wendell's mom. "They give you heartburn. Wendell, honey, do you want some more feet?"

"No thanks, ma." Wendell was still pretty full from his midnight feast.

Like every morning, the "It's Way Too Early to Be Awake" news show was on the kitchen TV. And like every morning, Wendell ignored whatever boring things the reporters were blabbing about. But then one news reporter started blabbing about something that wasn't boring at all:

"I am standing on the steps of City Hall," began news reporter Arturo Artery, as he brushed a giant flop of hair over a shiny bald spot on top of his head. "And man is it early in the morning! Why are you wolves up watching TV now anyway? If I were you, I'd be wrapped up in some snuggly blankets, burying my head in a cozy cave of soft pillows. But I'm out here freezing my butt off, so I might as well tell you the news: the police are going to be issuing a public safety warning about the cooked food monster any minute!" The camera panned over as the doors of City Hall flew open and a very serious-looking Detective Sam Slay marched to a podium.

"As most of us know by now," began Detective Sam Slay, "a burglary was committed at Wolf It Down Cafe last night."

"Did you catch the wolf who did it?" interrupted Arturo.

The Detective snarled. "No, we didn't catch the wolf who did it."

"Then why are we here? What gives? What are you hiding?!" continued the reporter.

"Hey baldy, zip it! The head scientist from our crime lab will explain everything if you stop asking a million questions!" yelled Slay.

Arturo covered the bald spot on his head with his microphone. "Breaking news: you're a meany," he whimpered.

Scientist Dr. Percy Pierce emerged from the building and walked up to the microphone. "We had a major breakthrough. The bad guy thief cut his hand on the broken window of The Wolf It Down Cafe. Our scientists analyzed the blood the thief left behind and..." Percy could barely say the next words.

"And what? What are you hiding?" shouted Arturo.

Finally, the scientist got up his courage and announced: "The blood was half-wolf, half-human! The cooked food monster is hiding amongst us!"

The crowd of reporters gasped. Camera flashbulbs popped. News reporter Arturo Artery's few remaining hairs popped off his head.

Detective Sam Slay stepped in front of the scientist and spoke directly into the news camera. "Half-Human, if you are out there watching, know this: I also found your footprint in freezer frost. It's only a matter of time until we, er, use science stuff to find you. I will hunt you down. You can run, but you can't hide forever."

Watching it all on his TV, Wendell dropped his spoon and gasped.

"Wendell, dear," asked his mother, "are you okay?"

Wendell answered by fainting face-first into his bowl of Shredded Mini Feet.

Wendell's dad looked up from his newspaper. "See? Wendell is upset about the fat cat tax, too!"

25

CHAPTER 6
A LOAD OF BULLY

That day at school, Wendell was worried, frightened, terrified, fearful and any other word you can think of that means scared out of your mind. When his best friends Benny, Robbie, and Roger Rabid offered him a nibble of the kindergartener's pet hamster, his stomach was too flippy-floppy to eat (which is not like his stomach at all). He felt like at any moment, the cops were going to bust down the doors and nab him. It was all he could think about. That's why when his math teacher, Ms. Gory, asked, "Wendell, what does 3 times 3 equal?" he answered, "I'm innocent!"

All the wolves in his math class busted out laughing. "Maybe the cooked food monster fried and ate Wendell's brain!" shouted Mike Maul from the back of the room.

Ms. Gory slammed a paw on her desk. The class froze in silence. "That is not funny! Don't you dare joke about an evil monster walking our streets!"

"How does anyone know it's evil?" asked Erin Eek from behind a flop of hair in front of her face. "Everyone gets in such a panic in this town if something is 'weird' or 'different.'"

"Of course Freak Girl thinks it's cool to be a monster!" laughed Mike.

"Enough!" scolded Ms. Gory. "Eating cooked food is not 'cool.' It is sick and twisted. But don't worry, whoever–or whatever–did this will be caught and will be locked in jail where they will rot away for..." She quickly typed some numbers into her calculator. "...a gazillion years, if my math is correct. So, you can all rest easily tonight...after you complete problems 1 through 25 at the end of Chapter 18. And I don't want to hear any moaning!"

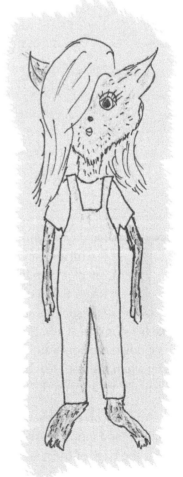

The bell rang, but you could barely hear it above all of the moaning. Wendell would have joined the homework moaning too if he wasn't too busy moaning about sitting in a jail cell for the rest of his life.

He wandered down the hall to his next class but was so consumed with his worried thoughts that he walked straight into Erin Eek.

"Oh, sorry!" exclaimed Wendell.

"It's okay. Are you feeling alright?" asked Erin.

"Sorta...ish," answered Wendell. "Hey, do you really think that the food eater running around town is cool?"

"I didn't say it was 'cool.' I just think it is so lame that whenever something is different around here, everyone goes nuts. I mean–ouch!"

Erin looked around to see who just shot her with a rubber band. School bully Mike Maul's annoying laugh rang out.

"Gee, sorry, must have slipped," he said.

"You're such a loser," Erin said.

Mike loaded up another rubber band and let it fly at her. Wendell, who was small, but super quick, blocked it with his notebook.

"Cut it out, Mike!" Wendell yelled.

"Make me cut it out, wimp," threatened Mike.

Oh boy, thought Wendell. He knew he had a lot of problems to deal with, but getting pounded by Mike Maul wasn't on his "need to worry about" list.

"Come on, Weenie Wendell," mocked Mike, "I said make me cut it out."

"No," answered Wendell.

"Why not, because you're a chicken?"

"No, because I'm going to knock you on your butt before Wendell gets a chance," announced Benny from behind Mike.

Mike spun around to find his buddy Benny flanked by Roger and Robby Rabid. Benny, it should be noted, was one of the biggest and strongest wolves in the whole school.

"You're not trying to pick a fight with our best pal Wendell, are you?" asked Benny.

"Oh, hey guys…no, I just, uh…" stammered Mike.

"Because when you mess with him, you mess with all the members of The Bite Club!" roared Benny, showing him the fake Magic Marker tattoos they each had drawn on their arms.

"Wow," squeaked Mike. "You have wonderful penmanship and, uh…I gotta go!" He turned to run but tripped over the janitor's mop and fell face-first into a disgusting bucket.

"You didn't have to do that, guys," said Wendell to his pals.

"Of course we did," answered Benny, "No one is allowed to pound you but me!" Benny, Roger and Robby all piled on Wendell, laughing and punching him in the arm.

"I'll see you in history class, Wendell," said Erin over the squealing maniacs rolling around on the hallway floor. "Thanks for telling that jerk

Mike to buzz off. That was sweet of you."

"No problem," said Wendell. He started to blush but no one could tell because Benny was now sitting on his head.

CHAPTER 7
FAMILY SHAME NIGHT

Wendell spent so much time worrying that today was going to be the worst day of his life that he forgot that it was also his favorite day of the month: Family Game Night. Every month, the kids would stay after school to play games in the gym. Their parents would come to join in the fun after work. Things weren't all bad, right?

Wrong! Tonight's game was square dancing, which Wendell found more painful than getting a strep throat test. Luckily, he got partnered up with his friend Erin, and none of the parents were there yet to make a fuss about "how cute!" they all looked dancing together.

Just as they were about to doe-see-doe, Ms. Incisor, the science teacher/dance instructor decided to make things more exciting.

"Spotlight Dance!" she shouted. The lights in the gym went dark and a dramatic spotlight trained itself directly on Erin and Wendell. They both froze in place.

"Come on, wolves," she cheered," Let's hear it for our spotlight couple!"

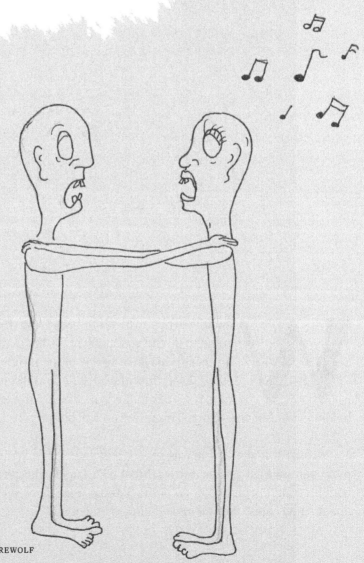

All the other kids started clapping. Wendell couldn't believe it. He woke up feeling like a monster and now he was being treated like a superstar!

He twirled Erin, showing off some of the moves he learned from watching his mom's favorite show "Dancing with the Zombies." The crowd went crazy!

"And now for the big finale," announced Ms. Incisor. "Everyone look up and let's get ready to howl at the moon!"

She pushed a button on the gym wall and with a rumble, two large panels on the roof began to slide back. The opening panels revealed a sliver of black sky, then some twinkling stars, then–oh no!–the bright glowing full moon!

The crowd cheered. Wendell gulped.

He shut his eyes as tight as he could. Maybe if he didn't see the moon, he wouldn't change?

After a minute, he opened his eyes and found the crowd staring at him. They were all chanting something. It sounded like "Groovin'! Groovin'!" But they didn't look exactly happy. In fact, they looked pretty unhappy. He listened harder and realized they were actually shouting "Human! Human!"

Wendell looked at his paws. They weren't paws anymore–they were smooth, disgusting fleshy hands. He touched his face. No whiskers. No wet nose. No sharp teeth...no luck.

Erin stared at him in shock.

"I'm sorry," he whispered to her.

He turned to the chanting crowd. "Please don't be afraid. It's just me, Wendell. Don't worry, I won't–"

Wendell was cut off his an extremely loud boom! He looked down

a saw a smoking slingshotted silver ball sticking out of the floorboards two inches away from his feet.

"Freeze! Don't move!" screamed Detective Sam Slay as he climbed down a ladder from the roof. "I knew I'd find you here! The crime lab had matched the footprint we found in the freezer frost to a person/wolf about the size of an 11-year-old!"

He began excitedly climbing down a ladder. "It wasn't much to go by, but I had a hunch you'd be here so I staked this dance out. I'm a genius!"

A genius who didn't really know how to climb down a ladder. A few steps down, Slay slipped and fell 15 feet down straight on his butt. The fall loosened Slay's grip on his slingshot, which sent another silver ball flying, which hit the rope holding up Ms. Incisor's "Howl at the Moon" sign, which sent it crashing to the ground, which caused everyone in the gym to run for their lives.

Taking advantage of the chaos, Wendell pulled his jacket over his head and zipped to the back door. He kicked it open and darted out into the night. Escape! Erin was shouting something to Wendell, but he couldn't make out what she was saying. And even if he did, he wasn't stopping for anything.

He raced across the kickball field and into the woods, leaving the school and the shrieks of terror behind. He ran as fast and as far as he could. Normally, Wendell felt like he was having a heart attack if he had to run more than the 50-meter dash in gym class, but fueled by fear, he ran for miles and miles all night. As the morning sun started to rise, he finally came to a stop when he felt a splash on his wolf feet. Wendell looked up. He was standing on the shore of the dreaded Fog Lake.

He'd never actually seen it before. Ever since he was a young wolf, he'd been told to stay away, that this was the most dangerous place in Eeeville. Humans lived on the other side–not good! But this morning, he felt like it was the only place in the world that was safe. Unfortunately for him, that safe feeling was about to go away very quickly.

Chapter 8
Hair Today, Gone Tomorrow

Know why they call it Fog Lake? Because it is really, really foggy. (Sorry, wish there was a more interesting answer.) You can only see about 10 feet in front of you and then there is just a wall of gray, mysterious mist.

Wendell stared out into the creepy grayness and was definitely feeling freaked out. He looked at his reflection in the water and thought about his friend Erin. Was he crazy, or did he remember her saying "It's okay" to him while everyone else was going nuts?

The wind kicked up, and Wendell saw the tip of something sticking out of some bushes. He scrambled over and checked it out. It was wood. It was long – it was a rowboat! Wendell figured that it must have been left here

by that traveling salesman Joe because there was a map inside that led to a place across Fog Lake called Manville.

Wendell realized he had two options: Go back home and try to explain to the town that he wasn't a monster and that they definitely didn't need to be put in jail for a gazillion years. Or he could jump in this rowboat and leave his troubles (and friends and family) behind.

Before he could think too much, a loud voice hit him like a fistful of sand. "Come on kid, stop running so I can lock you up!" Detective Sam Slay came stumbling out of the bushes. He had chased Wendell all the way from the school and was gasping for air. A detective trench coat and loafers are not ideal running clothes. And not doing any exercise for the last 30 years wasn't helping him much either.

Lock me up? For once, his brain and his stomach agreed on something: get in the boat! The rest of Wendell's body was onboard – literally – as he pushed the boat into the water, jumped in, and started paddling like crazy.

"Please stop?" begged Slay. "I'm exhausted!"

"Leave me alone!" Wendell shouted. "I didn't do anything wrong!" He was fighting the tide to get away from the shore but was struggling to make headway.

"Actually, you did do something wrong! You stole and cooked food," declared Slay. "Doesn't get any wronger than that."

"I can't help it," explained Wendell, furiously paddling but still getting nowhere. "I don't want to want

cooked food, but I can't stop the Tummy Rumbles."

"I don't know what a Tummy Rumble is, but here is one way to stop it – and everything else." Slay loaded a silver ball into his slingshot and sent it zipping through the air at poor Wendell.

The good news? Wendell wasn't hit – yay!

The bad news? His boat was – yipe!

The double-bad news? Wendell's boat finally caught the tide and quickly got pulled away to from the shore just as ice-cold water began gushing through the freshly-made hole.

Wendell yelped. He tried to reverse direction and paddle back, but the fog on Fog Lake was so thick Wendell couldn't tell which direction the shore was anymore.

"Come back criminal!" shouted Slay.

"I'm trying but I can't tell which direction to go!" replied Wendell.

"You're voice is echoing all over the place!"

"Oh cool, like in a cave?" asked Slay unhelpfully.

The boat was going down fast. Even with his thick wolf fur, Wendell didn't think he could last very long in that frigid water. (Besides, he forgot his arm floaties and wasn't the world's best swimmer.) For like the tenth time in the last 24 hours, Wendell was doomed. He pinched his nose as the water started coming up to his neck. A tear ran down his face and all he could do was whimper, "Mama?"

"Arrr, they'll be no mamas coming to yer rescue!" came a voice from the thick fog.

"Huh?" said Wendell.

"It sounds as if ye need help escaping this perilous puddle," answered the voice.

"Yes! Ye does need help! Ye does!" yelled Wendell.

He was pretty sure the cold water was freezing his brain and making him hallucinate, but it beat drowning so he decided to just go with it.

"Pledge yer undying loyalty to the captain of this pirate ship and ye shall be saved."

"I pledge, I pledge! Now please get me out of here!" Wendell begged.

A life preserver tied to a rope flew out from the fog and bonked Wendell on the nose. Wendell read the name on the life preserver. "S.S. Good Ship Lollipop?"

"Arr, I've been meaning to change that. Not a very pirate-y sounding name for a ship. But I just can't seem to find the time. The life of a pirate is a very busy one. Lots of chores and whatnot."

Wendell slipped the preserver over his head just as his rowboat sank to the bottom of Fog Lake. With a few mighty tugs, he was pulled aboard the S.S. Good Ship Lollipop. Wendell shook the ice-cold water off himself and caught his breath. He asked politely for a towel and prepared to begin living the life of a dastardly pirate.

CHAPTER 9
WORLD'S WEIRDEST PIRATE

The S.S. Good Ship Lollipop didn't look much like a pirate ship. Instead of a mighty sail, it had a puny little motor. And instead of canons, it had a pair of water skis. And the pirate captain? He didn't look like a pirate captain at all. He was wearing sandals, a pair of sunglasses and a tank top. Oh yeah, and he was human.

"My name is Captain...um, you know, I haven't come up with a pirate name yet, to be honest."

Wendell was confused about a lot of things happening at this moment but mostly wondered why this human wasn't flipping out about the talking wolf he just pulled up on his boat.

"Hi, I'm Wendell. Thanks for saving me."

"No worries, First Mate Wendell! Ah, see that sounds so cool. I need to get me a zinger of a name like that."

"Why don't you just pick a name?"

"It's not the pirate way. Most pirates are named after their beards, but arr, I haven't shaved in four months and this is all I have to show for it."

The pirate captain leaned forward to show two puny whisps of hair sticking out of his chin.

"Or they get named after some awesome freaky injury they're lucky enough to have, like having a hook for an elbow or something," he continued.

"Well, I've never seen a pirate wear sunglasses before," noted Wendell. "Maybe you can name yourself Captain Shades."

The pirate paused. He grunted. Then finally spoke in a low, gravelly whisper: "Captain Shades? Is that what ye'd have the world call me?!"

"Sorry, I just thought–"

The pirate leaned in close to Wendell. "The only thing you have to be sorry about is giving me the coolest name on Earth and not keeping it for ye self! Captain Shades, I love it! Put 'er there, ol' chum!"

Captain Shades stuck out his hand, but before Wendell could shake it, the Capatin turned and asked, "Hey, have you seen a pirate sword laying around here?"

"No," said Wendell. "Did you misplace it?"

"These shades are really dark, I can barely see anything," said the Captain. "And there's also the possibility that I never had a pirate sword to begin with! Memorizing things isn't really in the pirate skill set."

"I hope you don't mind me saying this," said Wendell, "but you don't look like the pirates I've seen in books and movies."

"Arr, the secret is out then," said Captain Shades. "Captain Shades wasn't always a bloodthirsty pirate. I just wanted to be the captain of a party boat in my hometown of Manville, but the fools who hand out licenses told me no."

"I don't understand."

"Either do I! How can you deny a dude a license to party when he's got moves like this?"

Captain Shades pressed the play button on his dashboard radio and speakers started thumping and bumping. Wendell wished he was wearing mittens so he could stuff them in his ears. The music was crazy loud. Captain Shades dove onto the floor and started breakdancing. It was the wildest dance routine Wendell had ever seen – arms and legs were flying everywhere. And in perfect time with the music, it ended with the Captain spinning on his head.

"Wow!" cried Wendell.

Captain Shades stood up proudly. "No one can rock a party like Captain Shades does. So when they told me I couldn't pilot my own ship because I failed the boat license test 37 times in a row, I stole one and hit

the open seas and never looked back."

"I totally understand," said Wendell.

"Good!" shouted Captain Shades. "Well, enough of this lip flapping. What's say we find us an adventure!"

"I say we do!" shouted Wendell.

The engine roared, waves broke over the bow and dreams of daring exploits filled Wendell's heart.

CHAPTER 10
THE ADVENTURE BEGINS!

The S.S. Good Ship Lollipop bopped along through the water, swayed from side to side, and did basically what you'd expect a boat to do. Oh, and a seagull flew by once. Also, Wendell scratched his butt. Other than that, nothing really happened.

CHAPTER 11
WAIT, YOU CALL THAT ADVENTURE?

N o, but how about this? The day after that, Wendell saw a monster's head sticking out of the deep mysterious waters of Fog Lake! Pretty exciting, right? Well, okay, sorry that didn't actually happen. But Wendell did see a cloud shaped like a football. That's kinda exciting, right? Didn't think so.

CHAPTER 12
SOME ADVENTURE PLEASE? PRETTY PLEASE?

J ust like you, Wendell was starting to get the feeling that life on this pirate ship was going to be a serious snore. But at least no one was shooting silver balls at him – that was a major plus. So he just sat there as Captain Shades drove the boat around in circles. Wendell had no idea where they were going, but he did know that he was getting seriously dizzy.

"Captain Shades, do you keep barf bags on board?"

Captain Shades immediately turned off the engines. "Sorry, the Captain forgot that you're not used to battling these fierce waters. If you want to lay down, there be an air mattress down below the poop deck. Oh and don't be grossed out by the name 'poop deck.' There be no pooping there. There be a porta-potty on the dingy we're towing behind us. If ye need to let one rip, let Captain Shades know and he'll pull the dingy in."

"That's okay, I'm feeling better. A little hungry, though," said Wendell.

"Don't worry, me hardy, ye will not go hungry on Captain Shade's boat. Gaze upon me treasure chest of granola bars!"

Captain Shades kicked over a cardboard box, spilling about a hundred foil-wrapped granola bars on the deck. "Dig in! There's more where that came from. The Captain does enjoy his bulk shopping!"

He gave a hardy laugh. Wendell unwrapped a banana-walnut bar and bit in. It tasted like a sawdust-covered banana that fell into a tub of glue. But he was starving so he choked it down. His stomach stopped rumbling,

but then he felt something else aching inside him: his heart. He missed his home. He missed cracking jokes with his friends. He missed his mom telling him to turn off the TV and to do his homework. Heck, he missed his homework!

"I miss homework? I must be crazy," Wendell thought.

But then he saw Captain Shades talking to a fish about starting a bowling team together, and thought, "Okay, maybe I'm not that crazy."

Later that night, through the fog, Wendell noticed the moon. It had been several weeks since the school dance, and the moon was almost full again. He looked down at the treasure chest of granola bars. They were not going to cut it when he turned human and the Tummy Rumbles came.

"Captain Shades?" asked Wendell. "You don't happen to have any cheeseburgers on board, do you?"

"Nopesy dopesy doodle," answered the captain. "Sick of the granola bars, are ye? Aye, the captain is too. Last night I had a nightmare that I was wrapped in foil and a giant banana was eating me – twasn't pleasant for me or the banana, I'll tell you that! But alas, we will have to wait patiently for a cargo ship transporting fast food to attack before we can sink our teeth into some yumminess."

"What if instead of waiting, we went looking for yumminess? The boat I was paddling when you rescued me had a map in it," said Wendell.

"A treasure map?"

"No, a map to Manville. Maybe they have cheeseburgers there?"

"Manville? I never heard of it!" barked the Captain.

"I thought you just said you are from there," asked Wendell.

"No, I didn't."

"Yes, you did. I heard it with my own two ears."

"Well, get your ears checked out because they aren't working so good, First Mate."

"Good idea!" said Wendell. "I'll bet there's an ear doctor in Manville who can fix me up."

"We're not going to Manville!" shouted Captain Shades. "All there are in that place are people who tell you that you can't pursue your destiny to be a party boat captain, so forget about it!"

Wendell was quiet for a minute, then asked, "Do you ever miss your friends and family?"

"Ah lad, that is the worst of it. I do miss me girlfriend Maureen."

"You left a girlfriend behind?"

"Well, I'm not sure she's what you'd technically call a 'girlfriend,' but she squeezed my hand during a scary part of a movie once. That's gotta mean something, right?"

"Totally! So you've never gone back, not even once?"

"I swore an oath that I'd sail this ship until the day I died. Or the boat sank, in which case I'd probably die. This water is, like, super deep. But until that day, I–"

"Freeze!" boomed a voice over a megaphone.

Wendell jumped down just as a spotlight hit Captain Shades in the face.

A booming voice came from the darkness: "This is the Manville Harbor Police. You are piloting a stolen boat. Put your hands on your head, turn off your motor and prepare to be boarded," declared the harbor policeman.

Wendell crawled on his belly and slipped down below deck.

The Captain wasn't sure how to put his hands on his head and turn his motor off at the same time, so he just stood there, crying. Nope, things were not looking so good for the pirate crew of the Good Ship Lollipop.

CHAPTER 13
SHOCK AND PAW

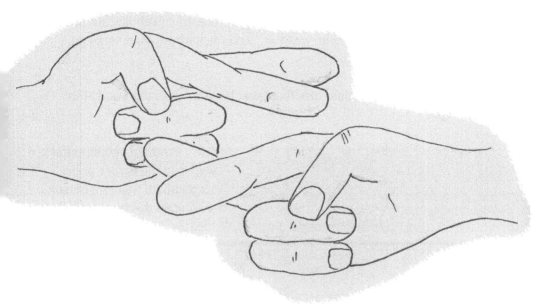

From his hiding spot down below, Wendell couldn't see what was happening. But he could hear everything.

"You are under arrest for stealing this vessel," explained the harbor police sergeant to Captain Shades. "Is there anybody else on this ship?"

The captain paused. "Ar, no, the captain sails alone!"

"Do you swear?"

"Yes!" replied the Captain.

"And you're telling the truth?" asked the harbor police sergeant.

"Aye! Swearsies!"

"Then why are your fingers crossed behind your back?" asked the police sergeant.

"Dang it!" exclaimed Captain Shades. "Foiled by me own fingers!"

"If you're going to play it like that, you leave me no choice but to unleash my most fearsome weapon," said the harbor police sergeant. "Bring out Officer Sniffers!"

Wendell heard a giant drooling beast hop on board the Good Ship Lollipop.

"He's a trained people sniffing dog," said the harbor police sergeant. "If there's a person hiding on this boat, he'll find 'em."

Sniffing dog? Wendell suddenly wished that he had showered more this week. Or at least used some deodorant.

"Go to work Officer Sniffers!"

Wendell listened as the big oaf of a dog ran around the deck sniffing, knocking over fishing poles and whatever else got in his way. Then he heard very loud chewing.

"Officer Sniffers!" shouted the harbor police sergeant, "Put those granola bars down! Bad officer, bad!"

"Arr, me treasure!" cried the Captain. "Get that creature off me ship!"

"This isn't your ship," said the harbor police sergeant. "Go check down below, Sniffers."

Officer Sniffers bounded down the stairs. Wendell crouched down in his hiding spot. He watched as Officer Sniffers gave a powerful sniff, then walked over to the air mattress.

Wendell was sure he was finished. Then Sniiffers let out a big yawn, and plopped his giant butt down on the mattress and instantly began snoring.

What's going on? thought Wendell. Why isn't Sniffers tearing me limb from limb? Then it hit him – Sniffers was a people-sniffing dog. And it wasn't a full moon, so Wendell was still a wolf. He wasn't people! Phew!

The harbor police tied a rope around the motor of the S.S. Good Ship Lollipop and towed it through the water. Twenty minutes later, the boat stopped moving with a giant thud. It was docked. In Manville. Wendell was now in human country.

CHAPTER 14
NEW YUM CITY

A fter the harbor police finished securing the S.S. Good Ship Lollipop to the dock, they secured Captain Shades in the back of a police wagon with a tight-fitting pair of handcuffs. "Buckle up, buddy," said the police sergeant. "We're taking you straight to your new home – jail!"

After the wagon pulled away, Wendell worked up the nerve to slink off the boat to take his first look at this new country filled with humans.

It was incredible! Wendell was amazed by the sights he saw, the sounds he heard and, mostly, the smells he smelled. At the far edge of the dock was a restaurant where a bunch of humans ate cooked food out in the open like it was the most normal thing in the world. Fries, chicken fingers, nachos – heaven! Suddenly ditching Eeeville seemed like the best idea ever. Who needs friends and family when you have greasy food to gobble? But before he could enjoy a single nibble, he needed to save the guy who saved him. Tonight, Wendell vowed, he'd bust Captain Shades out of jail.

CHAPTER 15
THE FARTY BOYS

It was pretty dark out, so Wendell had no problem using his wolf skills to sneak around town unnoticed. After a few hours wandering around streets and cutting through back alleyways, he finally found The Manville Jail. It was a giant cement building covered in bars and barbed wire. "How am I going to get in there and bust Captain Shades out that?" he thought. He climbed on top of a Dumpster in the alleyway to get a better view. Oof, it looked even bigger and scarier.

"Hey you!" said a human voice.

Wendell spun around to find a group of five human boys, about his own age, standing in the alleyway.

"Isn't it a little early to be wearing your Halloween costume?" asked one of the boys, mistaking Wendell's actual wolf body for a fake one.

Wendell thought quickly. Noticing that they were wearing jackets over pajamas, he shot back, "Well, isn't it a little late for you to be outside when your parents think you're asleep at your sleepover party?"

"Maybe," said the boy. "But we don't care. We're daredevils!"

"Well, I'm a daredevil, too," answered Wendell, jumping down from the Dumpster. "That's why I'm wearing my Halloween costume too early and staying outside too late!"

"Cool!" exclaimed the biggest boy named Reggie. "Can you do this?" Reggie stuck his hand under his armpit, squeezed, and made a remarkably realistic farting noise. The gang busted up laughing.

"Wow," gasped Wendell, "That is the most amazing thing I've ever seen in my whole life." (Remember: this is coming from a kid who grew up in a town of talking werewolves.)

"Wanna learn how to do it?" asked Reggie.

"No thanks, I'm too busy planning how I'm going to bust my friend out of jail," Wendell said.

"Bust your friend out of jail?" said Reggie. He looked at his buddies, then they all shouted together, "Awesome! Can we help?"

"Totally!" exclaimed Wendell. "Meet me back here tomorrow night. Wear black clothes and thick gloves," he said. Wendell looked up at the razor-sharp wires surrounding the jail. "And bring extra juice boxes. I have a feeling this is going to be a tough mission."

CHAPTER 16
TO EAT A MOCKINGBIRD

The next morning in Manville, Wendell woke up in his hiding place, which way up in a tree across the street from the jail.

After a breakfast of some newly hatched birds (gosh, did Wendell miss how his mom made them with the beaks cut off) he began planning Captain Shade's daring escape. And his great plan was...he didn't have one. The bars on the windows, the barbed wire, the guards walking around – Wendell thought breaking into this joint without an army tank would be impossible.

But he couldn't give up – he refused to! Captain Shades didn't leave Wendell to sink to the bottom of Fog Lake and Wendell wasn't going to leave Captain Shades in some stinking cell. There had to be a way to get him out! That's when he noticed all of the people walking in and out wearing "visitor" stickers on their shirts and jackets. Wendell thought for a minute. A full moon was due any night now. Could it be as easy as waiting to become human, then simply walking in the front door? He could hide some lock-picking tools under a jacket and pass them to Captain Shades when the guards weren't looking. It was so simple it had to work!

Except for the fact that it wouldn't work. Wendell got a closer look and saw that the guards asked all of the humans for IDs and made them walk through a metal detector. He didn't have an ID, and the metal detector would find the lock picks. Dang it!

Wendell didn't know what to do. Then he heard a dog barking and suddenly got a great idea. A totally awesome, super-duper fail-proof plan! He couldn't wait to tell his new human friends. He just needed to get down from this massive tree and he suddenly remembered that he was terrified of heights.

CHAPTER 17
HAIRY PLOTTER AND THE CAPTAIN'S ESCAPE

When Wendell finally got down from the tree, he met up with his human pals and explained his daring plan. Most of them thought it was crazy, but Reggie thought it would work. Which is why, three hours later, Reggie stepped up to the visitor's desk at the Manville Jail and told the guard, "I'm here to see my Uncle."

"Sorry, kid," said the prison guard behind the front gate. "No kids allowed."

Reggie pretended to start crying.

"Please!" Reggie begged through fake sobs, "It's going to break his heart if I don't show up. He's expecting a visit from me and his pet dog Rover!"

The guard looked over his desk and saw Wendell on all fours, wagging his tail.

"That is one weird-looking dog. What breed is that?" asked the guard.

"A, um, wolfydoodle. Half wolf, half poodle," lied Reggie. "He doesn't shed. Great for allergies and no mess on the furniture."

"Well, sorry for you and your...wolfydoodle, but rules are rules," stated the guard.

"Please? My uncle misses Rover so much!" Reggie started fake crying so hard, he actually started crying for real.

Standing in line behind Reggie and Wendell was a mountain of a man with the word PAIN tattooed on his forehead. "Hey kid, I might look like a criminal. Heck, I might actually be a criminal, but I have feelings. And your story was like a swift kick directly in the feelings." The mountain of a man with PAIN tattooed on his forehead bent down and scratched Wendell behind the ears. "You wanna go see your friend in there, little fella? I'm going inside to visit my Grandma. She has a bad habit of stealing Ferraris. I'll take you with me."

Wendell wanted to exclaim, "Thanks!" but he remembered that dogs aren't supposed to be able to talk, so he gave his best happy bark instead. "Ruff ruff!"

The mountain of a man with PAIN tattooed on his forehead took the leash, and just like that, Wendell walked on all fours into the Manville County Prison. "It's all going great!" thought Wendell. "Now whatever you do, don't swallow the lock pick hidden under your tongue!"

CHAPTER 18
CHICKEN SOUP FOR THE HALF-HUMAN SOUL

The visitor's center at the jail was filled with tables, like in a lunchroom. All kinds of people sat and talked with all kinds of prisoners. It was loud and crowded – the perfect scenario for a breakout. The mountain of a man with PAIN tattooed on his forehead unhooked Wendell's leash. "Go find your master, little wolfdoodle," he wept. "Go give him a big slobbery lick!"

Wendell scurried off. He searched and searched the room but couldn't find Captain Shades anywhere.

"Ten minutes left for visitors hour!" announced one of the guards. No! Wendell thought. Could it be that the captain isn't here?

"There is no Captain here!" said a voice.

Wendell spun around. The voice was coming from a man in a suit. And the man was seated at a table across from...Captain Shades! But instead of his tank top and flip flops, Captain Shades was wearing prison stripes!

"Arr, I be the Captain! Captain Shades be me name!"

"No," insisted the guy in the suit. "Your name is Carl. You aren't a pirate. You're my friend. We've been best friends since third grade, remember?"

"Aye, perhaps your face is starting to jog the Captain's memory," said Captain Shades.

"Well, look dude, you got everyone at the boat company mad when you stole that boat, but the whole town has been worried sick since you disappeared."

"Really?" squeaked the Captain, sounding less like a pirate than usual.

"Yes, really. Poor Maureen cried for days when they gave up the search for you."

"Maureen? Holy wowsers! She missed me?"

"Yes! And the party boat guys were so happy that you were found in one piece that they'll drop the charges," said the guy in the suit. "All they want is an apology and a promise that you'll never do it again. As your friend and your lawyer, I'm begging you to stop with this pirate stuff. Just be yourself. Just be Carl and everything will be okay. Can you do that?"

Captain Shades jumped up from his seat and hugged the man in the suit. "Aye aye–I mean, yes! Yes! Thanks for being such a great friend!"

Wendell couldn't believe it. Tears of joy dribbled down his face. The captain was going home! He was so happy for his friend.

Wendell thought about the Captain and Carl's conversation as he walked back to the visitor's entrance: So a dude who made a lot of people angry and was being hunted by the police was forgiven. All he had to do was apologize and agree to stop pretending to be someone he really wasn't. If it worked for Captain Shades, could it work for him, too? If he went back to Eeeville and apologized, maybe everyone would be so happy to see him that they'd welcome him back, too!

Reggie was waiting for Wendell outside.

"So, how did it go? Did you get him the lock pick? Is he going to bust out? Tell me everything that happened!"

"It went perfectly. Better than I expected, but I'm kind of exhausted right now," said Wendell. "You and the guys meet me by the Dumpster tonight at midnight. I'll tell you the whole story."

But when the guys showed up behind the Dumpster that night, they didn't find Wendell. Instead they found a note taped to the rusty container.

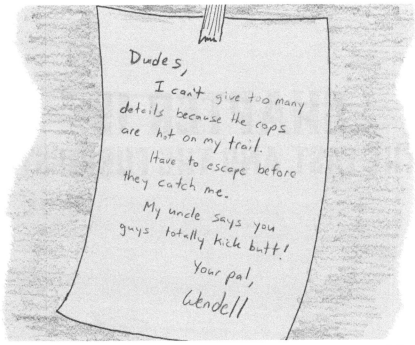

Dudes,

I can't give too many details because the cops are hot on my trail.

Have to escape before they catch me.

My uncle says you guys totally kick butt!

Your pal,
Wendell

At the exact moment that the guys were reading his note, Wendell was in the middle of committing his last crime in human country: he was untying a rental rowboat that he definitely had not rented. He jumped in and under the cover of night, started rowing into the icy waters of Fog Lake. Next stop: Eeeville.

He felt bad for lying to his human buddies, but he thought it was better for them to think that they busted out a law-breaking pirate instead of trying to explain that he was actually a wolf who turned into a human who craved cheeseburgers during the full moon. Which would you believe anyway?

CHAPTER 19
THE FAST AND THE FURRIEST

After rowing for three solid days and nights, Wendell's boat hit ground on the shore of Eeeville. His feet were happy to step on dry land, and his butt was furious for having to sit on a wooden bench for 72 hours straight.

"Sorry butt," Wendell said. His butt didn't say anything back, thankfully.

So what now? Should he go straight home and give his parents a giant hug? Or march into the center of town and announce he was back?

"Darn it, what should I do?" he asked his butt. (Note: those stuck in rowboats for extended periods of time tend to talk to their butts a lot.) "If only I had a sign!"

Then something nailed to a tree caught his eye. It was a sign! A note, actually. It read:

> Dear Wendell,
>
> By now you're probably hundreds of miles away. But if you ever do come back, I figured out a trick to hide your cooked food problem from everyone.
>
> If you want to know the trick, light off one of the flares I left hidden behind this tree. That will be the signal for me to meet you at the school gym at midnight. We can put my plan in motion and fix everything. I hope to see you soon!
>
> Your friend,
>
> Erin Eek

Wendell was so excited! He quickly found the hidden flare gun, pointed it into the night sky and squeezed the trigger. A bright orange burst lit up the sky and the trees around him. Wendell stared as it floated above, a beautiful glow at the end of this dark trouble-filled tunnel. He smiled and hoped that Erin saw it, too.

Erin didn't see it. But the wolf who actually left the note and the flare gun – the wolf who stayed up all night, night after night, scanning the northern skyline for the sign that the monster returned – saw it. The wolf's name? You might have guessed it: Detective Sam Slay.

CHAPTER 20
BRIGHT LIGHT, BIG TROUBLE

Slay almost peed himself with excitement when he saw the flare streak across the sky. He just knew that the monster would return. He knew it in his bones! Criminals always return to the scene of the crime. Case in point, just last year, he nabbed the Eeeville Savings & Loan bank robber standing in the middle of the bank – he was taking a selfie with his own wanted poster.

Detective Slay signed the note from "Erin" so that he could trick Wendell into going to the gym, where a trap waited for him. The plan was sure to work, but before Slay could put it into action, he needed to make sure none of Wendell's friends or family would get in the way. So to keep them quiet, he gave his police wolves a long list of wolves to throw in jail.

"Don't we need, like, a legal reason to arrest someone?" asked Officer Rita Roar.

"Make something up, like their teeth are too pointy," answered Slay.

First up to get tossed in the slammer: Wendell's parents.

"What do you mean my teeth are too pointy?" yelled Wendell's Dad through the bars of his jail cell. "Yours are even pointier!"

Officer Roar quickly covered up her smile. "I don't make the laws, sir, I just enforce them," she said, happily going back to work on her crossword puzzle book.

"Absurd!" huffed Wendell's dad. "If that's why you have me in here, why was my wife arrested too? This makes no sense. Does this have anything to do with my son Wendell? Have you found him? Is he okay?"

"The cooked food monster? Nope," lied Roar. She looked up from his crossword puzzle at the heartbroken parents. "Hmm, I need a nine-letter word that starts with the letter 'i'..."

"Our son is no monster!" shouted Wendell's mom. "We love him! This is an injustice!"

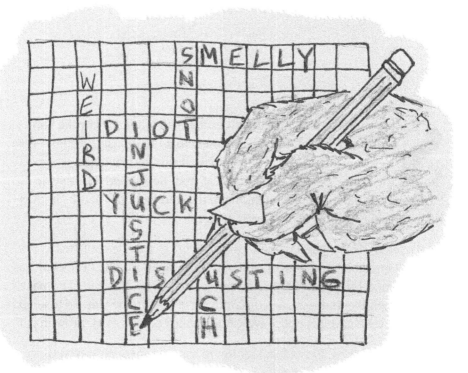

Roar looked up thoughtfully. "You know what? You're right."

"You mean you're going to let us out of here?" asked Wendell's dad.

"No, the word 'injustice,'" she said holding up her puzzle book. "That's the nine-letter word I was looking for! Thanks!"

Next, Detective Sam Slay's police wolves arrested Erin Eek. She was in the middle of taking her favorite barrettes out of her hair as they busted into her room. When she asked why she was being hauled off to jail, they told her that she square danced with the human-monster, and therefore might have caught his human cooties.

She tried to protest, but they threw her in the back of the cop car before she could assure them she had all of her vaccinations, which had to include cootie shots, right? Next, they arrested the wolves most likely to give Wendell a helping paw: his best buddies Benny, Robby, and Roger. And then just to be safe, they arrested anyone whose name started with the letter W.

When all the arresting was done, Detective Sam Slay put out a town-wide announcement that every wolf not currently in jail needed to go to the school gym at 8 P.M. for an emergency meeting. And to make sure the wolves actually showed up, he lied and said there would be free McDeadly's Unhappy Meals (with free barf bags in every box!)

Slay desperately wanted to capture Wendell by himself and be the big hero, but Wendell had gotten away from him too many times. Slay figured that if every wolf in Eeeville was ready to attack when he showed up to the gym, there was no way the cooked food monster was going to get out alive.

CHAPTER 21
A HAIRY SITUATION

The wolves of Eeeville arrived at the gym and were instantly annoyed that there weren't any Unhappy Meals waiting for them.

Slay took the microphone in the announcer's booth and boomed, "The cooked food monster is back!"

The wolves quickly shifted from complaining to panicking.

"And unless you help me stop him, we'll all be in terrible danger. First, he cooked a cheeseburger – maybe next he'll try to cook your brains!"

The crowd gasped.

"We are all doomed!" moaned Lenny Licker.

"We are all doomed?" asked Barry Blood. "I thought we were all wolves. Sheesh, I should have paid more attention in biology class."

"No, dummy," said Lenny Licker, "He means we're in trouble."

"We're in trouble?" asked Barry Blood. "I thought we were in a gym. I should have paid more attention during basketball practice."

"Barry! Can you zip it for 5 seconds and let me finish?" asked Detective Sam Slay.

"Finish? I thought you were Norwegian," said Barry. "Okay, I'll stop talking now."

"Thank you," said Slay. "Now, you will all notice that in the center of the gym, there are several wooden crates. They are filled with slingshots and silver balls. Now, here's the plan.."

Slay explained how he had left the fake note for Wendell to come to the gym at midnight. They would all hide with loaded slingshots and wait for the secret signal.

"I know I'm not supposed to talk anymore," said Barry. "But quick question: what's the secret signal?"

"Um, er," said Slay scratching his noggin. He knew he forgot something when he was coming up with this plan! "Uh, I guess the secret signal will be me jumping up and screaming, 'Get him!' That's when all of you shoot your slingshots at him. Got it?"

"Got it!" replied all of the wolves. Wendell was about to get it, too.

CHAPTER 22
DON'T GO IN THERE!

It was 11:55 PM. Five minutes to midnight. Wendell stood about 100 feet away from the back door of the gym. The moon was full and under its pale blue glow, he had once again taken human form. But he didn't care. All of his worries about getting caught were gone. Erin's note promised that she figured out a trick to hide his problem from everyone – and she was the smartest wolf in school.

But as he waited for his watch hands to tick midnight, something started to bother him. Did he really want to "trick" everyone and keep living this secret life?

No, he decided, he was sick of doing that. Trying to hide his humanness was the thing that got him into all of this trouble in the first place. Wendell decided that if he wanted to solve his problem, he'd have to confront it openly and honestly. He looked down at his watch. Midnight. He grabbed the gym door handle, pulled it open and whispered, "Erin, are you in there?"

She wasn't, but hiding in the dark were 300 wolves all with slingshots pointed straight at him

(Hey Wendell, next time maybe read the chapter heading before you do something. It clearly says "Don't Go In There!")

As Wendell crept into the darkness, his eyes began adjusting. What were all of the silver things glinting?

The lights flicked on. And Wendell had has answer: 300 silver balls pointed at his head.

"Cooked food monster, move to the center of the gymnasium!" commanded Detective Sam Slay.

Wendell did as he was told. He was hoping that he was dreaming, that everyone in his town wasn't really seconds away from blasting him, but that familiar scent of smelly gym socks made him realize that this was all very real.

"On the count of three, blast him!" barked Detective Sam Slay.

"One, two–"

Wendell wanted to yell, "Stop!" but before he could move his lips, someone else yelled, "Stop!"

It was Wendell's science teacher, Ms. Incisor. "Let's not attack him," she pleaded.

"Great idea!" said Wendell.

"Instead, we should perform all kinds of weird and gross experiments on him for fun," said Ms. Incisor. "And you know, for science."

"Horrible idea!" yelped Wendell.

"Yeah, horrible idea," agreed Barry Blood. "Science gives me a headache with all of those important dates and stuff."

"Isn't history the one with the dates?" asked Sheldon Shred. "Or it that geometry? I can never remember if George Wolfington was a president or a triangle."

"I've got a great compromise," declared Daisy Deadly. "Let's just stop talking and eat him!"

There was a quick discussion amongst the crowd, who all decided that it seemed like a good enough idea. The wolves closed in on Wendell, fangs ready to dig in.

Wendell could feel their hot, dank breath as they swarmed around him. "Wait, please! You don't understand! I'm nice, I'm not a monster! I didn't choose to be human, it's just who I am. I know I am different, but can't you accept me?"

"Oh jeez," said Barry Blood, "Not only is this kid a cooked food eater, but he's also a corny sap!"

"Let's eat him before he gives another boring speech!" yelled Dave Deadly.

The crowd moved in on him. Closer, closer, closer – then a voice came from the back of the gym.

"If you all are so hungry, why don't you eat this!"

Every wolf spun around to find Erin Eeek standing in the gym doorway, holding up a tray with a bag on it. She emptied the bag to reveal a half-eaten cheeseburger. The crowd shrieked in horror.

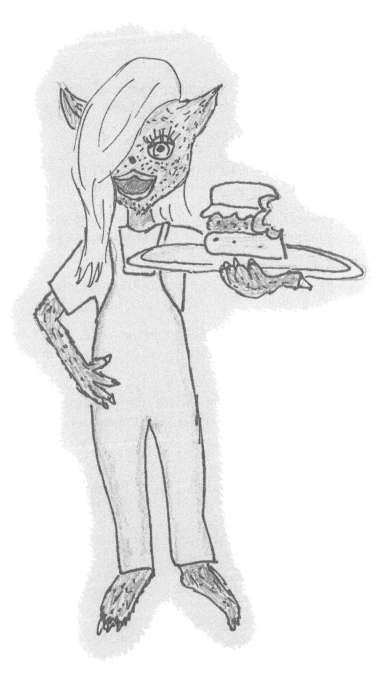

Detective Slay was confused and annoyed. "I am annoyed and confused," he said. "What are you doing?"

"When your police wolves arrested me, they didn't even give me a chance to finish taking my barrettes out of my hair – which was good because I used one to pick the lock on my jail cell. And also pick the lock to the evidence room, where I found this, Wendell's so-called crime." She jabbed the cheeseburger toward the crowd and they jumped back, pressing themselves against the gym walls.

"Are you crazy? Put the cheeseburger down before anyone gets hurt," commanded Detective Slay, slowly approaching her with handcuffs hidden behind his back. "We don't want anything bad to happen here. The adults would just like to capture and eat your friend."

"Oh, I don't think you're going to be hungry for Wendell tonight, Detective Slay," grinned Erin.

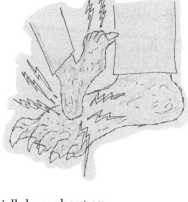

"Oh I think I will," said Detective Slay, who was now inches from Erin. He patted his belly. "I haven't eaten since breakfast."

"Well, how about an appetizer then?"

Before Slay could respond, Erin stomped his paw as hard as she could. Slay howled in pain.

Without a second to spare, Erin grabbed the cheeseburger and shoved it straight into Slay's open mouth.

Before he could think, he swallowed it.

The crowd gasped. Detective Slay grabbed his stomach in horror.

"Are you okay?" asked Ricky Rip.

Detective Sam Slay looked up. "No, I'm not okay," he said. "I'm...fantastic! That was the most delicious thing I ever ate!"

Wendell was instantly run over as every wolf rushed to try to get a lick of the tray the cheeseburger was on. Then everything went black.

He woke up to find Erin fanning air in his face.

"Am I dead?" asked Wendell.

"Nope," she said. "You just passed out. I pretty much just saved your life. No biggie."

"Yes biggie!" he exclaimed. "Big fat biggie! Thank you!" He leaped to his feet and gave her a huge hug. Then he suddenly got embarrassed. Then he suddenly didn't care and hugged her again.

Wendell had so much he wanted to say to Erin, but it was hard to say anything over the yelling and screaming of all the wolves fighting over the cheeseburger plate.

"Guys, don't fight!" he said. "If you want, I can make a fresh batch of burgers for everyone!"

The crowd cheered and their bellies growled. They lifted Wendell up on their shoulders and marched down to The Wolf It Down Cafe, where Wendell and Slay set up a giant barbecue and made about 400 cheeseburgers for everyone to gorge on.

In-between burps, everyone agreed that not eating Wendell and eating his grilled goodies instead was the best idea they ever had. While everyone happily chewed, Detective Sam Slay turned to Wendell and handed him a ring of keys. "Why don't you head over to the jail and let out the rest of your friends and family. I'm sure they're dying to see you."

"Thanks," said Wendell, "But Erin is already down there letting everyone out with her hair barrette."

"Jeez, we gotta get better locks," said Slay. "Hey, Wendell? I'm really sorry about that whole chasing-you-around-and-trying-to-kill-you thing. No hard feelings, right?"

"No hard feelings," said Wendell. "Sorry I made you scream like a wimp in front of the other police wolves."

"Forget it," answered Slay. "Seriously, forget it. Because if you ever mention that again, I will throw you in jail."

Wendell laughed for the first time he could remember in a long, long time.

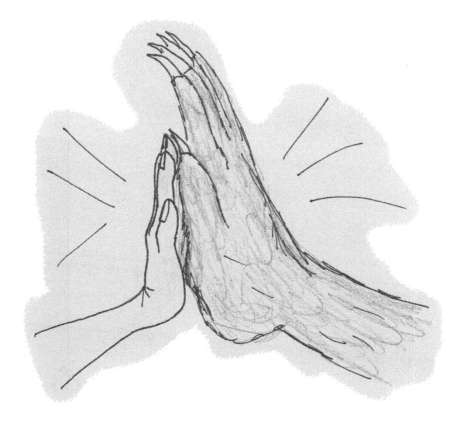

EPILOGUE
THE PART AFTER THE END

A fter Wendell's parents were busted out of jail, they ran over to the barbecue and hugged him so hard he bruised half of his ribs. Then his buddies Benny, Robby, and Roger bruised the other half.

He was surrounded by the wolves he loved, and they loved him right back. He couldn't believe it. A huge smile crept across his face and stayed there for the better of the day. And the day after that. And the day after that. And the day...well, you get the point. Let's just say that Wendell was a very happy cooked food monster.

Cooked food soon became all the rage in Eeeville, and after school, Wendell worked as the head chef in The Wolf It Down Cafe, now renamed Le Super Expensive Cafe. Eyeballs were replaced with meatballs, brains were replaced with broccoli and, of course, cheeseburgers became the most popular item on the menu. Wendell was cooking like a celebrity chef and getting better at it every day.

And it was a good thing that Wendell was sharpening up his culinary skills. Because little did anyone know, but just a few miles above Eeeville hovered the mothership of evil aliens, the Zytorgs. They were in the middle of a chili competition with their arch enemies, the Zylorgs, and they were about to demand that the wolves of Eeeville hand over a prize-winning recipe or get zapped by a giant laser cannon.

But that's another story for another book. For now, have a cheeseburger, burp and think twice about chasing someone away because they don't like to eat freshly scooped brains.

Made in the USA
Monee, IL
17 November 2022